Favorite NURSERY RHYMES *from*

MOTHER GOOSE

ALSO BY SCOTT GUSTAFSON

Classic Fairy Tales
Classic Bedtime Stories
Classic Storybook Fables

Favorite NURSERY RHYMES *from*

MOTHER GOOSE

Illustrated by SCOTT GUSTAFSON

Artisan | New York

ISBN 978-1-57965-698-0

Sources Consulted
The Annotated Mother Goose, William S. Baring-Gould and Ceil Baring-Gould, © 1967 The World Publishing Company; *The Oxford Nursery Rhyme Book*, Iona and Peter Opie, Oxford University Press, © 1955 Iona and Peter Opie; *Mother Goose*, arranged and edited by Eulalie Osgood Grover, Derrydale Books, © 1984 Crown Publishers, Inc.

Jacket front and back: *Mother Goose* (details)

Design by Bjorn Akselsen

For more information about Scott Gustafson's illustrations and books, please visit scottgustafson.com.

Artisan books are available at special discounts when purchased in bulk for premiums and sales promotions as well as for fund-raising or educational use. Special editions or book excerpts also can be created to specification. For details, contact the Special Sales Director at the address below, or send an e-mail to specialmarkets@workman.com.

Published by Artisan
A division of Workman Publishing Co., Inc.
225 Varick Street
New York, NY 10014-4381
artisanbooks.com

Artisan is a registered trademark of Workman Publishing Co., Inc.

Published simultaneously in Canada by Thomas Allen & Son, Limited

Printed in China

20 19 18 17 16

Contents

Little Bo Peep

Little Bo Peep has lost her sheep,

And doesn't know where to find them.

Leave them alone, and they'll come home,

Bringing their tails behind them.

Jack and Jill

Jack and Jill went up the hill,

To fetch a pail of water.

Jack fell down and broke his crown,

And Jill came tumbling after.

The Queen of Hearts

The Queen of Hearts
She made some tarts,
All on a summer's day.

The Knave of Hearts
He stole those tarts,
And took them clean away.

The King of Hearts
Called for the tarts,
And beat the Knave full sore.

The Knave of Hearts
Brought back the tarts,
And vowed he'd steal no more.

Jack *Be* Nimble

Jack be nimble,
Jack be quick,
Jack jump over
The candlestick.

Little Tommy *Tucker*

Little Tommy Tucker
Sings for his supper.
What shall we give him?
White bread and butter.

How shall he cut it
Without a knife?
How will he marry
Without a wife?

Wee Willie *Winkie*

Wee Willie Winkie
Runs through the town,
Upstairs and downstairs
In his nightgown.

Rapping at the window,
Crying through the lock,
Are the children all in bed,
For now it's eight o'clock?

Goosey,
Goosey,
Gander

Goosey, goosey, gander,
Whither shall I wander?
Upstairs and downstairs
And in my lady's chamber.

Humpty *Dumpty*

Humpty Dumpty sat on a wall,
Humpty Dumpty had a great fall.
All the King's horses and all the King's men
Couldn't put Humpty together again.

Little Tommy
Tittle*mouse*

Little Tommy Tittlemouse
Lived in a little house.
He caught fishes
In other men's ditches.

For want of a nail, the shoe was lost,
For want of a shoe, the horse was lost,
For want of a horse, the rider was lost,
For want of a rider, the battle was lost,
For want of a battle, the kingdom was lost,
And all for the want of a horseshoe nail.

Pussycat,
Pussycat

Pussycat, Pussycat,
Where have you been?
I've been to London
To look at the Queen.

Pussycat, Pussycat,
What did you there?
I frightened a little mouse
Under her chair.

Rub-a-Dub-Dub

Rub-a-dub-dub,

Three men in a tub.

And who do you think they be?

The butcher, the baker,

The candlestick maker,

Turn 'em out, knaves all three!

Ride a Cockhorse

Ride a cockhorse
To Banbury Cross,
To see a fine lady
On a white horse.

Rings on her fingers,
And bells on her toes,
And she shall have music
Wherever she goes.

Twinkle, Twinkle, Little Star

Twinkle, twinkle, little star,
How I wonder what you are!
Up above the world so high,
Like a diamond in the sky.

When the blazing sun is gone,
When he nothing shines upon,
Then you show your little light,
Twinkle, twinkle, all the night.

When the traveler in the dark,
Thanks you for your tiny spark,
He could not see which way to go,
If you did not twinkle so.

Jack Sprat

Jack Sprat could eat no fat
His wife could eat no lean,
And so between them both, you see,
They licked the platter clean.

Under a Hill

There was an old woman
Lived under a hill,
And if she's not gone,
She lives there still.

Baked apples she sold,
And cranberry pies,
And she's the old woman
That never told lies.

Polly Put the Kettle On

Polly put the kettle on,

Polly put the kettle on,

Polly put the kettle on,

Polly put the kettle on,

We'll all have tea.

Yankee Doodle

Yankee Doodle came to town,

Riding on a pony.

He stuck a feather in his cap

And called it macaroni.

Peter, Peter Pumpkin Eater

Peter, Peter pumpkin eater,

Had a wife and couldn't keep her;

He put her in a pumkin shell

And there he kept her very well.

Three *Blind* Mice

Three blind mice, see how they run!

They all ran after the farmer's wife,

Who cut off their tails with a carving knife,

Did you ever see such a thing in your life,

As three blind mice?

Bat, Bat

Bat, bat, come under my hat,

And I'll give you a slice of bacon.

And when I bake,

I'll give you a cake,

If I am not mistaken.

The North
Winds

Cold and raw the north winds blow
Bleak in the morning early,
All the hills are covered with snow,
And winter's now come fairly.

Little Jack Horner

Little Jack Horner

Sat in the corner,

Eating his Christmas pie.

He put in his thumb,

And pulled out a plum,

And said,

"What a good boy am I!"

Old *Mother* Hubbard

Old Mother Hubbard
Went to the cupboard,
To fetch her poor dog a bone.
But when she got there
The cupboard was bare,
And so the poor dog had none.

The Lion and the Unicorn

The lion and the unicorn
Were fighting for the crown.
The lion beat the unicorn
All around the town.

Some gave them white bread,
And some gave them brown.
Some gave them plum cake
And drummed them out of town.

Pat-a-Cake

Pat-a-cake, pat-a-cake,

Baker's man

Bake me a cake

As fast as you can;

Pat it and prick it,

And mark it with a T,

Put it in the oven

For Tommy and me.

Hickory,
Dickory, *Dock*

Hickory, dickory, dock,

The mouse ran up the clock.

The clock struck one,

The mouse ran down,

Hickory, dickory, dock.

Baa, Baa, Black *Sheep*

Baa, baa, black sheep,
Have you any wool?
Yes, sir, yes, sir,
Three bags full.

One for the master,
And one for the dame,
And one for the little boy
Who lives down the lane.

Hey
Diddle,
Diddle

Hey diddle, diddle,

The cat and the fiddle,

The cow jumped over the moon.

The little dog laughed

To see such sport,

And the dish ran away with

The spoon.

Old *Mother* Goose

Old Mother Goose,

When she wanted to w

Would ride through th

On a very fine gander

Scott Gustafson

Peter Piper

Peter Piper picked a peck
Of pickled peppers.
A peck of pickled peppers
Peter Piper picked.

If Peter Piper picked a peck
Of pickled peppers,
How many peppers
Did Peter Piper pick?

The *Itsy-Bitsy* Spider

The itsy-bitsy spider
Climbed up the waterspout.
Down came the rain
And washed the spider out.

Out came the sun
And dried up all the rain,
And the itsy-bitsy spider
Climbed up the spout again.

Mary *Had a Little* Lamb

Mary had a little lamb,
Its fleece was white as snow,
And everywhere that Mary went
The lamb was sure to go.

It followed her to school one day,
That was against the rule.
It made the children laugh and play
To see a lamb at school.

The Old Woman in the Shoe

There was an old woman
Who lived in a shoe,
She had so many children
She didn't know what to do.

She gave them some
Broth without any bread.
She whipped them all soundly
And put them to bed.

Little Miss Muffet

Little Miss Muffet
Sat on a tuffet,
Eating her curds and whey.
Down came a spider,
Who sat down beside her,
And frightened Miss Muffet away.

Fiddle-de-dee

Fiddle-de-dee, fiddle-de-dee,

The fly shall marry the bumblebee.

They went to the church, and married was she:

The fly has married the bumblebee.

An Old Woman

There was an old woman tossed up in a basket,
Seventeen times as high as the moon.
Where she was going I couldn't but ask it,
For in her hand she carried a broom.

"Old woman, old woman, old woman," quoth I,
"Where are you going to up so high?"
"To brush the cobwebs off the sky!"
"May I go with you?"
"Aye, by and by."

Old King Cole

Old King Cole
Was a merry old soul,
And a merry old soul was he.
He called for his pipe
And he called for his bowl
And he called for his fiddlers three.

Every fiddler he had a fiddle,
And a very fine fiddle had he.
Oh, there's none so rare
As can compare
With King Cole
And his fiddlers three!

Simple Simon

Simple Simon met a pieman,

Going to the fair.

Said Simple Simon to the pieman,

Let me taste your ware.

Said the pieman to Simple Simon,

Show me first your penny.

Said Simple Simon to the pieman,

Indeed, I have not any.

Sing a *Song* of Sixpence

Sing a song of sixpence,
A pocket full of rye.
Four and twenty blackbirds,
Baked in a pie.

When the pie was opened,
The birds began to sing.
Was not that a dainty dish,
To set before the King?

The King was in his countinghouse,
Counting out his money.
The Queen was in the parlor,
Eating bread and honey.

The maid was in the garden,
Hanging out the clothes,
When down came a blackbird
And pecked off her nose.

Hickety,
Pickety

Hickety, pickety, my black hen,

She lays eggs for gentlemen.

Gentlemen come every day

To see what my black hen doth lay.

Mary, Mary

Mary, Mary, quite contrary,

How does your garden grow?

With silver bells and cockleshells,

And pretty maids all in a row.

The Crooked Man

There was a crooked man,
And he walked a crooked mile,
He found a crooked sixpence
Against a crooked stile.

He bought a crooked cat,
Which caught a crooked mouse,
And they all lived together
In a crooked little house.

Little Boy Blue

Little Boy Blue,
Come blow your horn,
The sheep's in the meadow,
The cow's in the corn.

Where is the boy
Who looks after the sheep?
He's under a haystack
Fast asleep.

Will you wake him?
No, not I,
For if I do,
He's sure to cry.

The Man in the Moon

The man in the moon
Looked out of the moon
And this is what he said,
"'Tis time that, now I'm getting up,
All babies went to bed."

Index of First Lines

A Note from the Artist

The illustrator would like to thank the many friends and family members who graciously consented to being photographed while wearing silly hats and holding awkward poses. These photographs were an invaluable reference for many of the characters in this book, and I couldn't have done it without them. My models, in alphabetical order, were:

Hilary Barta; Jim Batts; Thomas Blackshear; Ajeya Brandon-Hopson; Andrew Cerf; Dominic Cielak; Kori Edens; Jack and Will Fineberg; Niki Gianni; Anthony Gonzales; Dorothy Gustafson; Patty and Karl Gustafson; Mary Jane Haley; Colin Jones; Sabina, Sean, and Zoë Kim; Edward Kuich; Mary and Jack Lahey; Hugh Martin; Jane Olson; Carol Renaud; Lena Reynolds; Rena Schergen; Henry Simpson; Benjamin Spenler; Mattuesz Stochelski; Cassidy Tucker; Charlotte Tyler; Kensey and Morgan Wallace.

Additional thanks to Wendy Wentworth, for her encouragement, expertise, and above all — patience. Also, to Scott Usher, who not only believed in, encouraged, and supported this project, but without whom it would not have happened.

Last, but not least, very special thanks to my lovely wife, Patty, for all the "behind-the-scenes" work, design consultation, computer wizardry, and moral support. And, to our son, Karl, for being a great kid.

Scott Gustafson